Geronimo Stilton
ENGLISH!

19 LET'S COOK! 入廚樂！

新雅文化事業有限公司
www.sunya.com.hk

Geronimo Stilton English
LET'S COOK!　入廚樂！

作　　者：Geronimo Stilton 謝利連摩‧史提頓
譯　　者：申倩
責任編輯：王燕參
封面繪圖：Giuseppe Facciotto
插圖繪畫：Claudio Cernuschi, Andrea Denegri, Daria Cerchi
內文設計：Angela Ficarelli, Raffaella Picozzi
出　　版：新雅文化事業有限公司
　　　　　香港筲箕灣耀興道3號東匯廣場9樓
　　　　　營銷部電話：（852）2562 0161
　　　　　客戶服務部電話：（852）2976 6559
　　　　　傳真：（852）2597 4003
　　　　　網址：http://www.sunya.com.hk
　　　　　電郵：marketing@sunya.com.hk
發　　行：香港聯合書刊物流有限公司
　　　　　香港新界大埔汀麗路36號中華商務印刷大廈3字樓
　　　　　電話：（852）2150 2100　傳真：（852）2407 3062
　　　　　電郵：info@suplogistics.com.hk
印　　刷：C & C Offset Printing Co.,Ltd
　　　　　香港新界大埔汀麗路36號
版　　次：二〇一二年二月初版
　　　　　10 9 8 7 6 5 4 3 2 1

版權所有‧不准翻印
中文繁體字版權由 Atlantyca S.p.A. 授予
Original title: CUCINIAMO!
Based upon an original idea by Elisabetta Dami
www.geronimostilton.com

Geronimo Stilton names, characters and related indicia are copyright, trademark and exclusive license of Atlantyca S.p.A. All Rights Reseved.
The moral right of the author has been asserted.

Stilton is the name of a famous English cheese. It is a registered trademark of the Stilton Cheese Makers' Association.
For more information go to www.stiltoncheese.com

No part of this book may be stored, reproduced or transmitted in any form or by any means, electronic or mechanical, including photocopying, recording, or by any information storage and retrieval system, without written permission from the copyright holder. For information address Atlantyca S.p.A., via Leopardi 8 - 20123 Milan, Italy - foreignrights@atlantyca.it - www.atlantyca.com

ISBN: 978-962-08-5495-8
© 2007 Edizioni Piemme S.p.A., Via Tiziano 32 - 20145 Milano - Italia
International Rights © 2007 Atlantyca S.p.A. - via Leopardi, 8, Milano - Italy
© 2012 for this Work in Traditional Chinese language, Sun Ya Publications (HK) Ltd.
9/F, Eastern Central Plaza, 3 Yiu Hing Rd, Shau Kei Wan, Hong Kong
Published and printed in Hong Kong

CONTENTS
目錄

BENJAMIN'S CLASSMATES
班哲文的老師和同學們

Maestra Topitilla
托比蒂拉・德・托比莉斯

Rarin
拉琳

Diego
迪哥

Rupa
露芭

Tui
杜爾

David
大衛

Sakura
櫻花

Mohamed
穆哈麥德

Tian Kai
田凱

Oliver
奧利佛

Milenko
米蘭哥

Trippo
特里普

Carmen
卡敏

Atina
阿提娜

Esmeralda
愛絲梅拉達

Pandora
潘朵拉

Takeshi
北野

Kuti
菊花

Benjamin
班哲文

Hsing
阿星

Laura
羅拉

Kiku
奇哥

Antonia
安東妮婭

Liza
麗莎

GERONIMO AND HIS FRIENDS
謝利連摩和他的家鼠朋友們

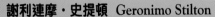

謝利連摩·史提頓 Geronimo Stilton
一個古怪的傢伙，簡直可以說是一隻笨拙的文化鼠。他是
《鼠民公報》的總裁，正花盡心思改變報紙業的歷史。

菲·史提頓 Tea Stilton
謝利連摩的妹妹，她是《鼠民公報》的特派記者，同
時也是一個運動愛好者。

班哲文·史提頓 Benjamin Stilton
謝利連摩的小侄兒，常被叔叔稱作「我的
小乳酪」，是一隻感情豐富的小老鼠。

潘朵拉·華之鼠 Pandora Woz
柏蒂·活力鼠的姨甥女、班哲文最好的朋友，
是一隻活潑開朗的小老鼠。

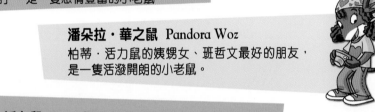

柏蒂·活力鼠 Patty Spring
美麗迷人的電視新聞工作者，致力於她熱愛的電視事業。

賴皮 Trappola
謝利連摩的表弟，非常喜歡食物，風趣幽默，是一隻饞
嘴、愛開玩笑的老鼠，善於將歡樂傳遞給每一隻鼠。

麗萍姑媽 Zia Lippa
謝利連摩的姑媽，對鼠十分友善，又和藹可親，只想將
最好的給身邊的鼠。

艾拿 Iena
謝利連摩的好朋友，充滿活力，熱愛各項運動，他希望
能把對運動的熱誠傳給謝利連摩。

史奎克·愛管閒事鼠 Ficcanaso Squitt
謝利連摩的好朋友，是一個非常有頭腦的私家
偵探，總是穿着一件黃色的乾濕樓。

A FABULOUS PRESENT
一份極好的禮物

　　親愛的小朋友，我是一隻幸運的老鼠，而且是超級幸運！你們知道為什麼嗎？看在一千塊莫澤雷勒乳酪的份上，因為我有一位非常會做菜的姑媽！沒錯，就是瑪嘉蓮姑媽啦！為了給我們一個驚喜，她今天帶了所有的材料來我家，要給大家做一頓美味大餐呢！班哲文和潘朵拉還邀請了他們的朋友一起來，真熱鬧啊！

跟我謝利連摩·史提頓一起學英文，
就像玩遊戲一樣簡單好玩！

你可以一邊看着圖畫一邊讀。
以下有幾個標誌，你要特別留意：

當看到 標誌時，你可以聽CD，
一邊聽，一邊跟着朗讀，還可以跟
着一起唱歌。

當看到 ★ 標誌時，你可以和朋友
們一起玩遊戲，或者嘗試回答問
題。題目很簡單，它們對鞏固你所
學過的內容很有幫助。

當看到 ! 標誌時，你要注意看一
下格子裏的生字，反覆唸幾遍，掌
握發音。

最後，不要忘記完成小測驗和練習
冊裏的問題！看看你有多聰明吧。

祝大家學得開開心心！

謝利連摩·史提頓

WHAT A LOT OF FOOD!
很多食物啊！

潘朵拉和班哲文都很想知道瑪嘉蓮姑媽的菜籃裏裝了些什麼，於是瑪嘉蓮姑媽把菜籃裏的食物一一拿出來給他們介紹，你也跟着一起說說看。

flour

tomato sauce

There is a lot of food!

pasta olive oil

bread

butter

rice sugar

eggs

milk

cheese yoghurt cocoa oatmeal

fresh vegetables honey

chocolate cornflakes

What is jam made of?

Jam is made of fruit and sugar.

a lot of food
很多食物

SNACK TIME　茶點時間

當瑪嘉蓮姑媽在做菜的時候，班哲文和潘朵拉準備了一些小食招呼他們的朋友。

some slices
of bread
數片麵包

Benjamin and Pandora
are preparing a snack
for their friends.

Benjamin gets some
slices of bread.

Pandora spreads jam on
the slices of bread.

The snack is ready:
everybody can eat!

What would you like to drink?

Water, please!

Sparkling water!

Some orange juice!

 試着用英語説出以下詞彙：蘇打水，橙汁。

答案：*sparkling water, orange juice*

 9

MY FAVOURITE FOOD
我最喜歡的食物

這天，賴皮剛好來到我家，他想讓大家知道他也是一個很出色的廚師！於是他向大家介紹他最喜愛的菜式！

Trappola's Menu

 spaghetti with tomato sauce

 roast chicken

  roast potatoes

 soup

 stew with potatoes

 French fries

 minestrone

 baked fish

 cheesecake

 four-cheese pizza

 mixed salad

 fruit salad

scrambled eggs

 grilled steak

 grilled vegetables

 lemon ice cream

A SONG FOR YOU!

 Track 1

My Favourite Food

Spaghetti with tomato sauce
four-cheese pizza
grilled steak or roast chicken.
Yummy yummy yummy!

Are you hungry?
Let's cook together!
It's so fun!
This is my favourite food!

接着，賴皮又逐一問大家愛吃什麼。

What do you like most, Geronimo?

I like four-cheese pizza, mixed salad and lemon ice cream.

I like spaghetti with tomato sauce and grilled steak.

I like roast chicken and roast potatoes.

I like stew with potatoes!

⭐ 你喜歡吃什麼呀？
參考賴皮的菜單，
用英語說説看。

I like... .

 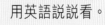

11

THE RECIPES　食譜

我以一千塊莫澤雷勒乳酪發誓，瑪嘉蓮姑媽的食譜看起來太吸引鼠了！不管是芝士包還是酸乳酪蛋糕都很好吃。我、班哲文和潘朵拉都很想學做芝士包和酸乳酪蛋糕，你也跟我們一起來做吧！

Cheese Buns

Ingredients　材料：

4 cups of flour　麵粉4杯
1 package of yeast　酵母1包
salt　鹽
rosemary　迷迭香
olives　橄欖
oil　油
cheese slices　片裝乳酪

Combine the flour with the yeast, a pinch of salt, half a cup of water and knead the dough.

Roll out the dough with the rolling pin. With a glass, cut out some circles of dough.

Put the buns on the greaseproof paper. Season them with a little oil, add some rosemary and a few olives.

Put a thin slice of cheese on each bun. Ask an adult to put them in the oven!

12

Yoghurt Cake

Ingredients 材料：

4 cups of flour   麵粉4杯

4 eggs   雞蛋4隻

$\frac{1}{2}$ cup of sugar   糖 $\frac{1}{2}$ 杯

a pinch of salt   鹽少量

1 spoonful of baking powder   發粉1匙

1 pot of yoghurt   酸乳酪1罐

1 cup of milk   牛奶1杯

1

I'm mixing all the ingredients.

Mix all the ingredients in a bowl until you have a soft mixture.

2

I'm putting the yoghurt cake in the oven.

Pour the mixture into a baking tray. Ask an adult to put it in the oven and leave it there for 20 minutes.

!

Pandora doesn't like cakes.
潘朵拉不喜歡吃蛋糕。

What does it taste like?
它是什麼味道的？

蛋糕終於焗好了，瑪嘉蓮姑媽把蛋糕拿出來分給大家吃。

What does it taste like?

It's very sweet!

Pandora doesn't like cakes very much!

CAKES ARE SWEET
蛋糕是甜的

　　有鼠喜歡吃甜甜的蛋糕，有鼠喜歡吃香噴噴的薄餅，有鼠喜歡喝淡味道的菜湯，可是沒有鼠喜歡太酸的味道……更重要的是，太燙或太冷的食物也是不太受歡迎！一起來看看下面這些食物到底怎麼樣吧！

Cakes are sweet.

Pizzas are savoury.

This minestrone is tasteless.

Lemon is sour.

This milk is too hot.

This steak is too cold.

 試着用英語說出以下句子：

1. 這牛奶太冷了。

2. 這碗意大利蔬菜濃湯太燙了。

14

答案：1. This milk is too cold.
2. This minestrone is too hot.

HEALTHY FOOD 健康的食物

　　瑪嘉蓮姑媽還向班哲文和潘朵拉介紹不同食物所包含的營養和功能，並叮囑他們一定要均衡飲食，這樣身體才會健康。

oil and butter

They contain fats that give a lot of energy, but watch out: you must eat them in small quantities. Extra virgin olive oil also contains vitamin E.

meat, fish, eggs, beans

They are rich in proteins, iron, fats, vitamin A and B. They are good for you!

fruit and vegetables

They contain sugars, fibres, minerals and vitamins. Citrus fruits are rich in vitamin C, which helps you get better when you have a cold.

bread, pasta, rice, potatoes

They contain carbohydrates, complex sugars that give you energy.

DINNER IS READY!
晚餐準備好了！

我以一千塊莫澤雷勒乳酪發誓，看到擺滿餐具的桌子真開心啊！好胃口立刻就來了！班哲文和潘朵拉又趁着這個機會學習各種餐具的英文名稱，你也跟着一起學習吧！

tablecloth　桌布
plate　碟子
saucer　茶杯碟
bowl　碗
glass　玻璃杯
fork　叉子
knife　刀子
spoon　匙子
teaspoon　茶匙
napkin　餐巾
salad bowl　盛沙律的碗
soup-tureen　湯鍋
oil and vinegar　油和醋
salt and pepper　鹽和胡椒粉
cup　杯子

I've just ...
我剛剛……
I've already ...
我已經……

Pandora, put the tablecloth on the table, please!

I already have, Uncle G!

I've just put the plates on the table.

And I've already brought the napkins!

I've just brought the mini-pizzas to the table!

A SONG FOR YOU!

 Track 2

Ten Green Bottles

10 green bottles hanging on the wall
and if 1 green bottle should accidentally fall
there'll be 9 green bottles hanging on the wall.
9 green bottles hanging on the wall
and if 1 green bottle should accidentally fall
there'll be 8 green bottles hanging on the wall.
8 green bottles hanging on the wall
and if 1 green bottle should accidentally fall
there'll be 7 green bottles hanging on the wall.
7 green bottles hanging on the wall
and if 1 green bottle should accidentally fall
there'll be 6 green bottles hanging on the wall.
6 green bottles hanging on the wall
and if 1 green bottle should accidentally fall
there'll be 5 green bottles hanging on the wall.
5 green bottles hanging on the wall
and if 1 green bottle should accidentally fall
there'll be 4 green bottles hanging on the wall.
4 green bottles hanging on the wall
and if 1 green bottle should accidentally fall
there'll be 3 green bottles hanging on the wall.
3 green bottles hanging on the wall
and if 1 green bottle should accidentally fall

there'll be 2 green bottles hanging on the wall.
2 green bottles hanging on the wall
and if 1 green bottle should accidentally fall
there'll be 1 green bottle hanging on the wall.
1 green bottle hanging on the wall
if that 1 green bottle should accidentally fall
there'll be no green bottle hanging on the wall.

I'M HUNGRY! I'M THIRSTY!
我的肚子餓了！我口渴了！

終於到了吃飯的時候了！瑪嘉蓮姑媽把做好的菜全部端了出來，放在飯桌上。我、賴皮、班哲文和潘朵拉已急不及待吃了起來！

在進食前，瑪嘉蓮姑媽還提醒我們要注意個人衞生和保持良好的飲食習慣，這樣身體才會健康。你也一起來學習吧！

Wash your hands before you eat!

Have snacks of vegetables and fruit.

Do not eat too many sweets: they contain sugars that damage your teeth.

Try to vary your food choices. Eat at least one portion of vegetables and fruit per meal.

When you eat, chew each mouthful thoroughly.

After eating, always brush your teeth.

〈一份有用的禮物〉
謝利連摩：我的報紙出版了一份新副刊——乳酪食譜，我感到很自豪。
瑪嘉蓮姑媽：真了不起！

潘朵拉：為什麼你邀請我們來廚房看呢？

謝利連摩：第一期副刊將會附送一份禮物。
瑪嘉蓮姑媽：你還未決定送什麼禮物？

謝利連摩：對極了！我想找一份最實用的禮物，例如：一個可以用來混合材料的大碗。

瑪嘉蓮姑媽：或者是一塊廚房用的抹布，可以用來抹手。

謝利連摩：不如我們一起來煮點東西，看看我們需要什麼。班哲文，把食譜遞給我。
班哲文：乳酪意大利粉！

謝利連摩：唔……非常簡單！把乳酪、鹽和胡椒放入碗中……

潘朵拉：看來一塊布不夠用來清潔所有的東西。

謝利連摩：呀，我全身都髒了……

潘朵拉：或許穿圍裙會比較好，不是嗎？

瑪嘉蓮姑媽：說得對！

潘朵拉：現在來做一個乳酪梳芙厘吧。

謝利連摩：好的！

謝利連摩：麵粉、牛油、牛奶……

謝利連摩：現在做甜品吧。
瑪嘉蓮姑媽：或許穿一條大圍裙會更好。

謝利連摩：現在做甜品吧。
瑪嘉蓮姑媽：乳酪蛋糕！
謝利連摩：好的！

謝利連摩：雲呢拿、朱古力、乳酪！

潘朵拉：謝利連摩叔叔，現在我們知道送什麼禮物給像你這樣的廚師最適合了。
謝利連摩：是什麼？

謝利連摩：一件連褲工作服！我看起來怎麼樣？
瑪嘉蓮姑媽：不錯，就像平時一樣！

The End

TEST 小測驗

⭐ 1. 用英語説出以下詞彙。

(a) 糖　　(b) 牛奶　　(c) 蜜糖　　(d) 可可　　(e) 牛油　　(f) 橄欖油

⭐ 2. 用英語説出以下句子。

(a) 你想喝點什麼？

What would you ... ... ?

(b) 請給我水！

..., ... !

⭐ 3. 讀出下面的菜式名稱，然後找出相配的圖畫，把代表答案的英文字母填在空格內。

A. grilled vegetables
B. baked fish
C. cheesecake
D. scrambled eggs

(a) ☐　　(b) ☐　　(c) ☐　　(d) ☐

⭐ 4. 讀出下面的句子，然後找出相配的圖畫，把代表答案的英文字母填在空格內。

A. They contain carbohydrates.
B. They are rich in vitamin C.
C. They contain fats.
D. They are rich in proteins.

(a) ☐　　(b) ☐　　(c) ☐　　(d) ☐

DICTIONARY 詞典

（英、粵、普發聲）

A

adult　成年人

apron　圍裙

B

baked fish　烤魚

baking powder　發粉

　　（普：泡打粉）

baking tray　焗盤

　　（普：烤盤）

beans　豆類食物

boiler suit　連褲工作服

bottle　瓶子

bowl　碗

bread　麵包

brush teeth　刷牙

butter　牛油

　　（普：黃油）

C

carbohydrates　碳水化合物

cheese　乳酪

cheesecake　乳酪蛋糕

chew　咀嚼

chicken　雞

chocolate　朱古力

　　（普：巧克力）

cocoa　可可

cold　冷／感冒

cornflakes　粟米片

　　（普：玉米片）

cup　杯子

D

damage　破壞

delicious　美味的

dessert　甜品

dough　麵團

drink　喝

E

eat　吃

eggs　雞蛋

energy　能量

F

fats　脂肪

fibres　纖維

flour　麵粉

food　食物

fork　叉子

French fries　薯條

fresh vegetables　新鮮蔬菜

fruit salad　雜果沙律
　　　（普：雜果沙拉）

G

glass　玻璃杯

green　綠色

H

healthy　健康

honey　蜜糖（普：蜂蜜）

hungry　肚子餓

I

ice cream　雪糕

ingredients　材料

invite　邀請

iron　鐵質

J

jam　果醬

K

kitchen　廚房

knead　揉（麵團）

knife　刀子

L

lemon　檸檬

like　喜歡

M

meat　肉

menu　餐牌（普：菜單）

milk　牛奶

minerals　礦物質

minestrone　意大利蔬菜濃湯

mini-pizza　迷你薄餅

mixed salad　雜錦沙律

　（普：雜錦沙拉）

must　必須

N

napkin　餐巾

O

oatmeal　麥片

oil and vinegar　油和醋

olive oil　橄欖油

orange juice　橙汁

oven　焗爐（普：烤箱）

P

pasta　意大利粉

pinch　少量

pizza　薄餅

plate　碟子

potatoes　馬鈴薯

present　禮物

proteins　蛋白質

R

recipes　食譜

rice　米

rolling pin　擀麪棍

rosemary　迷迭香

S

salad bowl　盛沙律的碗

　（普：盛沙拉的碗）

salt and pepper　鹽和胡椒粉

salty　鹹的

saucer　茶杯碟

scrambled eggs　炒蛋

season　調味

simple　簡單

snack　茶點 / 小食

soup　湯

soup-tureen　湯鍋

sour　酸的

spaghetti　意大利粉

sparkling water　蘇打水

spoon　匙子

steak　牛扒
　　（普：牛排）

sugar　糖

sweet　甜的

V

vitamins　維他命

W

wall　牆

watch out　小心

Y

yeast　酵母

yoghurt　酸乳酪

T

tablecloth　桌布

teaspoon　茶匙

thirsty　口渴

tomato sauce　番茄醬

today　今天

看在一千塊莫澤雷勒乳酪的份上，你學得開心嗎？很開心，對不對？好極了！跟你一起跳舞唱歌我也很開心！我等着你下次繼續跟班哲文和潘朵拉一起玩一起學英語呀。現在要說再見了，當然是用英語說啦！

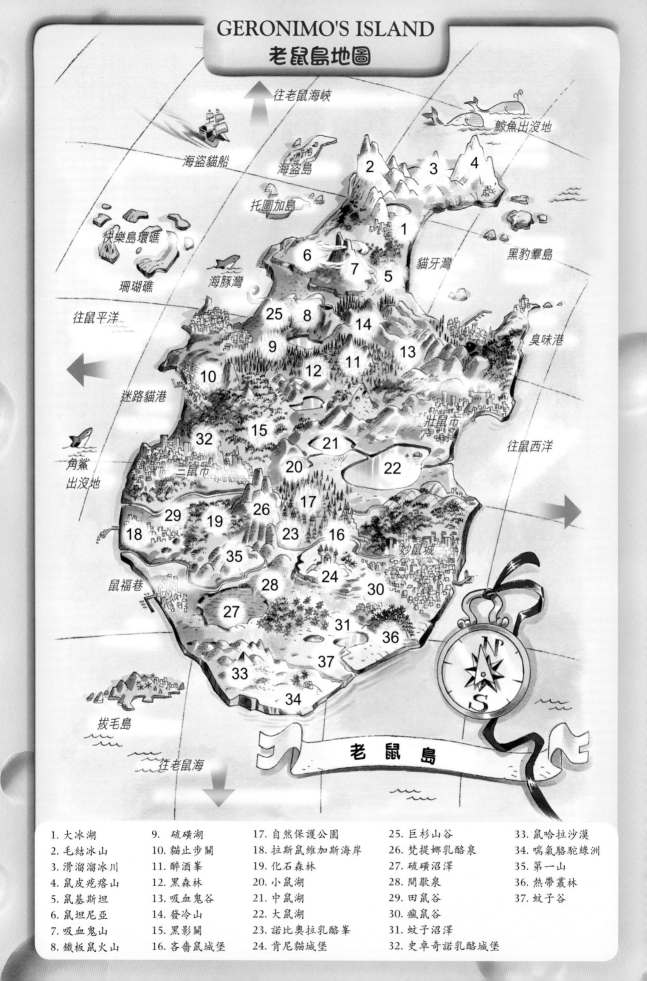

GERONIMO'S ISLAND
老鼠島地圖

往老鼠海峽

鯨魚出沒地

海盜貓船　　海盜島

托圖加島

快樂島環礁

珊瑚礁　　海豚灣

往鼠平洋

迷路貓港

角鯊
出沒地

鼠福巷

拔毛島

往老鼠海

貓牙灣

黑豹羣島

臭味港

壯鼠市

往鼠西洋

妙鼠城

三鼠市

老鼠島

N
S

1. 大冰湖	9. 硫磺湖	17. 自然保護公園	25. 巨杉山谷	33. 鼠哈拉沙漠
2. 毛結冰山	10. 貓止步關	18. 拉斯鼠維加斯海岸	26. 梵提娜乳酪泉	34. 喘氣駱駝綠洲
3. 滑溜溜冰川	11. 醉酒峯	19. 化石森林	27. 硫磺沼澤	35. 第一山
4. 鼠皮疙瘩山	12. 黑森林	20. 小鼠湖	28. 間歇泉	36. 熱帶叢林
5. 鼠基斯坦	13. 吸血鬼谷	21. 中鼠湖	29. 田鼠谷	37. 蚊子谷
6. 鼠坦尼亞	14. 發冷山	22. 大鼠湖	30. 瘋鼠谷	
7. 吸血鬼山	15. 黑影關	23. 諾比奧拉乳酪峯	31. 蚊子沼澤	
8. 鐵板鼠火山	16. 客嗇鼠城堡	24. 肯尼貓城堡	32. 史卓奇諾乳酪城堡	

Geronimo Stilton

EXERCISE BOOK
練習冊

想知道自己對 LET'S COOK! 掌握了多少，
趕快打開後面的練習完成它吧！

ENGLISH!

19 **LET'S COOK!** 入廚樂！

WHAT A LOT OF FOOD!
很多食物啊！

⭐ 瑪嘉蓮姑媽買了很多食物，你知道它們的英文名稱嗎？選出代表答案的英文字母填在空格內。

A. butter   B. eggs   C. pasta
D. yoghurt   E. fresh vegetables   F. bread
G. chocolate   H. cheese   I. honey
J. rice   K. olive oil
L. tomato sauce

1.  ☐

2.  ☐

3. ☐

4.  ☐

5.  ☐

6.  ☐

7.  ☐

8. 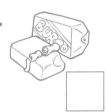 ☐

9. ☐

10.  ☐

11. ☐

12. ☐

SNACK TIME 茶點時間

⭐ 班哲文和潘朵拉正在準備一些美味的小食招呼他們的朋友。讀出下面的句子,把句子按他們準備小食的過程順序排好,然後在空格裏填寫代表答案的英文字母。

A. The snack is ready: everybody can eat!

B. Benjamin and Pandora are preparing a snack for their friends.

C. Pandora spreads jam on the slices of bread.

D. Benjamin gets some slices of bread.

☐ → ☐ → ☐ → ☐

2

TRAPPOLA'S FAVOURITE FOOD 賴皮最喜歡的食物

⭐ 下面這些都是賴皮最喜歡的食物。你知道這些食物的英文名稱嗎？在橫線上填寫缺少的字母，然後給圖畫填上顏色。

1.

lemon i__e cr__am

2.

spaghetti with __omato __ auce

3.

four-ch__ese p__zz__

4.

grill__d stea__

5.

ste__ with potato__s

6.

r__ast chicken

7.

mi__ed s__lad

8.

ro__st pot__toes

WHAT DO YOU LIKE MOST?
你最喜歡吃什麼？

⭐ 根據圖畫，從下面選出適當的詞彙填在橫線上，完成句子。

salad   vegetables   sauce   fish   fruit
roast   pizza   steak

1. I like four-cheese _____ , mixed _____ and lemon ice cream!

2. I like spaghetti with tomato _____ and grilled _____ !

3. I like baked _____ and grilled _____ !

4. I like _____ potatoes and _____ salad.

4

CAKES ARE SWEET
蛋糕是甜的

★ 根據圖畫，從下面選出適當的句子寫在橫線上，然後讀出句子。

This milk is too hot.　　Lemon is sour.
Pizzas are savoury.　　Cakes are sweet.

1.

_____

_____

2.

_____

_____

3.

_____

_____

4.

_____

_____

DINNER IS READY!
晚餐準備好了！

⭐ 晚餐準備好了！看看桌上放了些什麼餐具，從下面選出正確的詞彙填在空格內，然後給圖畫填上顏色。

bowl	glass	fork	plate	knife
teaspoon	spoon	tablecloth	napkin	

I'M HUNGRY! 我的肚子餓了！

⭐ 進食前，瑪嘉蓮姑媽提醒大家要注意個人衛生和保持良好的飲食習慣，身體才會健康。看看下面的圖畫，把圖畫和相應的句子用線連起來。

1.

A. After eating, always brush your teeth.

2.

B. Do not eat too many sweets: they contain sugars that damage your teeth.

3.

C. When you eat, chew each mouthful thoroughly.

4.

D. Wash your hands before you eat!

5.

E. Have snacks of vegetables and fruit.

ANSWERS 答案

TEST 小測驗

1. (a) sugar   (b) milk   (c) honey   (d) cocoa   (e) butter   (f) olive oil

2. (a) What would you <u>like to drink</u>?   (b) <u>Water</u>, <u>please</u>!

3. (a) D   (b) B   (c) A   (d) C

4. (a) B   (b) D   (c) C   (d) A

EXERCISE BOOK 練習冊

P.1

1. F   2. J   3. B   4. C   5. H   6. D   7. L   8. A   9. K   10. E   11. I   12. G

P.2

B→D→C→A

P.3

1. lemon i<u>ce</u> cr<u>ea</u>m   2. spaghetti with <u>t</u>omato <u>s</u>auce   3. four-ch<u>ee</u>se pi<u>zz</u>a   4. grill<u>e</u>d steak

5. ste<u>w</u> with potato<u>es</u>   6. r<u>oa</u>st chicken   7. mi<u>x</u>ed s<u>a</u>lad   8. r<u>oa</u>st pot<u>a</u>toes

P.4

1. pizza, salad   2. sauce, steak   3. fish, vegetables   4. roast, fruit

P.5

1. Cakes are sweet.   2. Pizzas are savoury.   3. Lemon is sour.   4. This milk is too hot.

P.6

P.7

1. E   2. D   3. A   4. C   5. B